S0-AIJ-859

For my brother and sis-by-marriage, Paul and Connie Schweigert.
Your love-in-action helped me carve out a new career path for myself
in Montana. Thank you, guys!

~ Sue Lawrence ~

For Mathias. How quietly you carved your way into my heart, sweet
nephew. Thank you for helping me bring Montana to life. I can't wait to see
what path you carve out for yourself in life—I know it will be incredible!

~ Erika Wilson ~

www.mascotbooks.com

Montana's Memory Day: a nature-themed foster/adoption story

For more information, please contact:
Mascot Books
620 Herndon Parkway, Suite 320
Herndon, VA 20170
info@mascotbooks.com

Library of Congress Control Number: 2021907135

CPSIA Code: PRT0521A
ISBN-13: 978-1-64543-460-3

Printed in the United States

MONTANA'S MEMORY DAY

a nature-themed foster/adoption story

SUE LAWRENCE

illustrated by

ERIKA WILSON

My name is Montana.
Tomorrow is my Memory Day.

I'm a thinker and a rememberer.

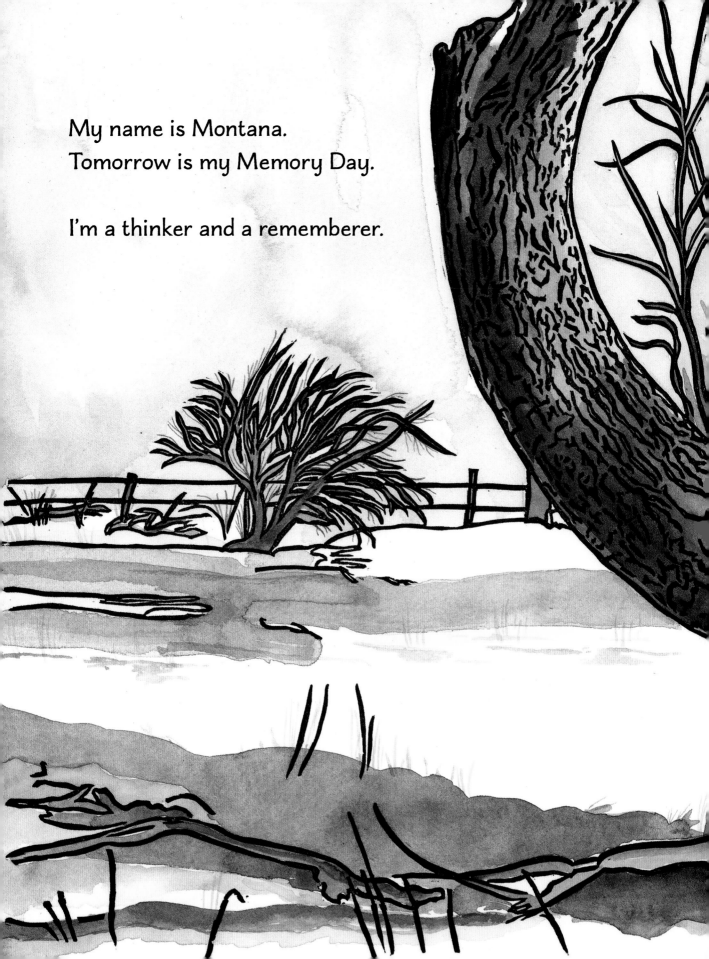

I used to change houses a lot.

Mixed-up feelings followed me from place to place.

But now I live with New Mom.
There's a differentness about this mom.
She's like a steady stream that gurgles.

She teaches me. There's always stuff to do around here. Today, we gathered firewood for the woodstove.

WHACK   CLUNK   THUD

I'm learning how to whittle.
I practice using one of
New Mom's old knives.
She says I'll make a good
carver one day, too.

CUT FLICK PEEL

I wish I had my own
knife to whittle with.

She wakes me at dawn to walk in the woods.

Our boots stomp the silence of the new-fallen snow.

CRUNCH
CRUNCH
CRUNCH

A wisp of white glides nearby, low to the ground.
"Whoa! What's that?"
"It's a snowy owl, hunting for breakfast."

Today looks different than yesterday did.
The snow sparkles like spilled glitter.

"This branch you found will be good for carving. Good job, Montana."
"Thanks. Let's walk the creek home."

An American dipper dives into the creek
and hops out with a bug in her beak.

SKIP DIP FLUTTER

A magpie flits his tail in a distant tree.
I think he's eyeing me.

"Are those wolf tracks?"
"No, they're too small for a wolf. These are
coyote tracks. But don't worry—
there's room here for all of us."

We stride to the farmhouse, side by side.

STOMP STOMP STOMP

Nature walks make me hungry.

"I'll make baked apples."

CORE   SPRINKLE   BAKE

New Mom stirs up a coffee cake.
A warm, cinnamon-sugar scent tickles my nose.

We remember our adoption day together.

I made her a surprise in art class.
"Oh, I love it! How quietly you carved your way
into my heart, Montana."
She gives me a box inside a box.

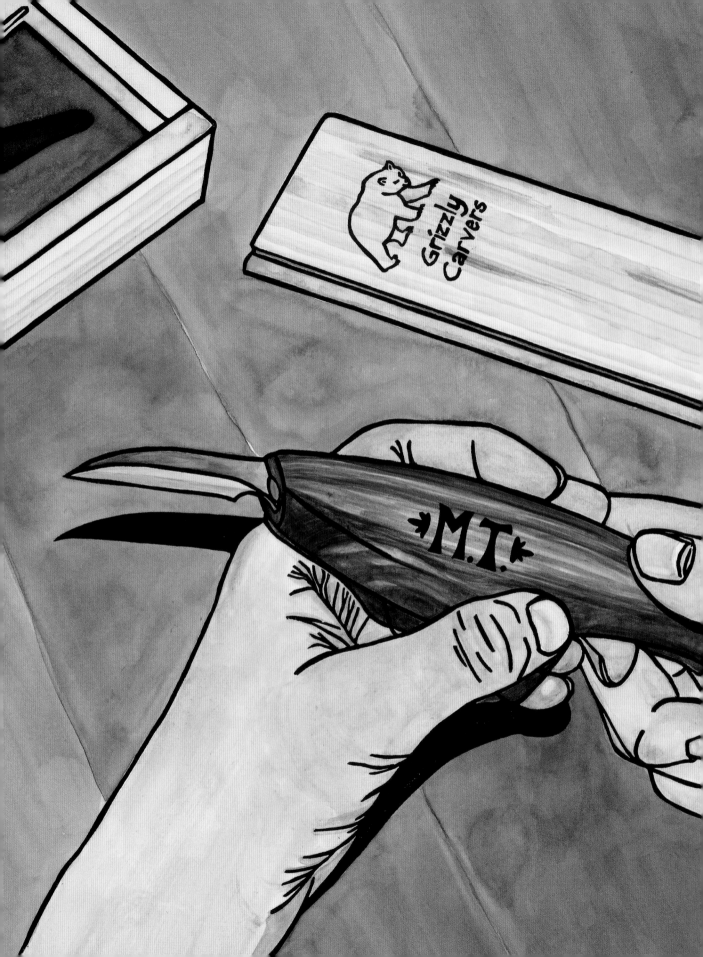

It's a carving knife!
My initials are etched into the handle like permanent ink.

This branch we brought home needs to dry out.
Then, I can carve it into whatever I want.

CARVE SHAPE CREATE

It's still early, but already
this is my best Memory Day.

THE ILLUSTRATION PROCESS

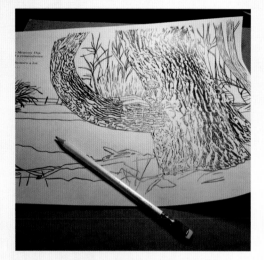

Tracing line drawing in graphite

Transferring image to lino block

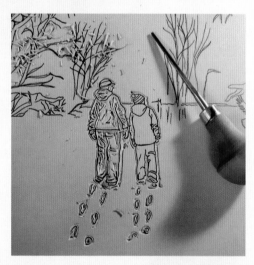

Permanent marker preserves image

Carving away all negative space

Inking block with brayer

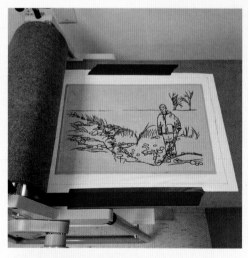

Printing block on etching press

ILLUSTRATOR'S NOTES

As soon as I read Sue's manuscript, I knew exactly how I wanted to illustrate this book. With the woodcarving element that winds through this story, I felt it was only fitting to bring it to life with hand-carved block prints. I was blessed to have the perfect setting–our family's Montana farm–all around me for inspiration. Also, I will be forever grateful to my dear nephew and sister-in-law for letting me take hundreds of pictures of them for reference photos for Montana and New Mom.

ERIKA WILSON is a Montana artist with two passions–children's book illustration and printmaking. *Montana's Memory Day* is her third picture book; she also illustrated *Skedaddle* and *The Spill*, both by Jacqueline Leigh. She is blessed to live with her family along the Yellowstone River outside of Billings, Montana. Whenever Erika isn't illustrating books, you can find her treadling an antique press in her letterpress print shop, The Windy Mill Press. For more information on her books or her letterpress, please visit:
erikawilsonart.com
windymillpress.com

Erika in her print shop

AUTHOR'S NOTES

I did not grow up in the foster care system, but I was married to two men who did. I wrote this story to give voice to an under-represented demographic in children's literature–foster kids and teens–and intentionally wrote it in the first-person point of view. I wanted you to hear Montana's thoughts, see his needs, and relate to his experiences as he learns to bond with yet another grown-up that has come into his life–his New Mom.

The boy in this story is named Montana, like the state, because it means "mountain" and "strength." Foster children have learned to be strong and resilient like a mountain range, yet still yearn for their own sense of identity. Family means the most to those who don't have one.

Photo by Marina Eshelman

Like Montana, I, too, carved out a new life for myself four years ago. After spending more than four decades as a Registered Nurse in America's Deep South, I switched gears and drove 1,900 miles in two days' time to do college a second time around. When I graduated from Rocky Mountain College at age 60, I was the oldest graduate to walk across that commencement stage–this time with a creative writing degree. I've kept my southern accent, but Montana is now my home. Its people are hardy, hard-working, and proud. Thanks for adopting me, Montana–I got here as quick as I could.

I'm an active Society of Children's Book Writers and Illustrators (SCBWI) member and volunteer for the Montana region. You can connect with me on Instagram:

@kidlitconnection @montanaexplorer @scbwimontana

My website is kidlitconnection.com.

WORDS AND PHRASES USED IN THIS STORY AND WHAT THEY MEAN

*Memory Day – A way to remember a special event again on that same date, every year.

*Rememberer – A deep thinker; someone who remembers events, usually in great detail.

*Differentness – Not the same as everyday; totally different from what you're used to.

"A steady stream that gurgles" – Steady means consistent, reliable. To gurgle means to bubble up, to be lively. The phrase here is a symbol for New Mom–she can be counted on to always be there for Montana, and she takes interest in what he does.

Whittle – To cut shapes or characters out of a wooden stick or a branch using a pocketknife, or a specially shaped carving knife–always with adult supervision.

Dawn – The early morning hour of the day when night fades out and the sun rises. Also known as "the golden hour" by photographers because the lighting is so good for nature photography.

Wisp – A tiny, quick glimpse of something.

Flits – A quick, on-purpose jerk of the black-billed magpie's foot-long tail feathers.

Eyeing – Looking intently, staring.

Stride – To walk quickly, with purpose.

Core - To cut out the center of the apple (where the seeds are) using a coring knife.

"How quietly you carved your way into my heart, Montana." – New Mom is telling Montana how much she has grown to love him. His place with her is secure as her forever son.

Etched – Etched means carved, like carving your initials into the bark of a tree. No matter how old the tree gets, your initials will always be there.

Permanent – It will stay there forever and ever.

"I can carve it into whatever I want." – This phrase has two meanings. Montana now has a carving knife of his very own, like he wanted, so he can start carving bigger things out of wood than he was doing before using little sticks. This phrase is also a symbol for his life and his future. He can carve–or shape it–as he chooses.

*These are not "real" words that you'll find in a dictionary. I made them up for this story. That's okay, though–you can make up new words in the stories you write, too.

RECOMMENDED READING

Foster Care and Adoption
- *No Matter What: A Foster Care Tale*, Written by Josh Shipp with David Tieche, Illustrated by Yuliya Pankratova. Published by Familius, 2020.
- *Speranza's Sweater*, Written by Marcy Pusey, Illustrated by Beatriz Mello. Published by Miramare Ponte Press, 2018.

Montana
- *Montana for Kids: The Story of Our State*, Written and Illustrated by Allen Morris Jones. Published by Bangtail Press, 2018.

Whittling and Carving*
- *The Stick Book: Loads of Things You Can Make or Do with a Stick,* Written by Jo Schofield and Fiona Danks. Published by Quarto Publishing, UK, 2012.
- *Forest Craft: A Child's Guide to Whittling in the Woodland*, Written by Richard Irvine. Published by Guild of Master Craftsman Publications, Ltd, UK, 2019.

*Although I used the terms "whittling" and "carving" interchangeably in this book for simplicity's sake, they are not the same thing. Woodworkers whittle small things using a stick; they carve larger shapes and objects from a branch, log, tree stump, or the bark of a tree. Children should always be supervised by an adult when learning how to whittle and carve. Safety equipment like hand gloves, thumb guards, and instructional videos are available online for beginners. Whittling is a forest-fun way for parents and kids to connect with one another.

FOSTER CARE ADOPTIONS: DID YOU KNOW?

The more I educate myself about foster care and foster care adoptions, the more I realize how much I didn't know before I began writing this book:

- There are over 437,000 children in foster care on any given day in the United States. The number one objective of foster care is to reunify these children with their parent(s) or another family member, and this happens almost half the time (49 percent). Of the remaining 51 percent, half are adopted. That still leaves more than 100,000 kids in the foster care system in limbo.*

- Kids and teens end up in foster care through no fault of their own. Their parent may have also been a foster kid or teen, too, who aged out of the system without being adopted into a caring family.

- Even after changing foster homes multiple times–which, of course, means a new school each time, too–some foster kids and teens excel in school and consider it their "safe space." Reading and learning empower children and teens to set and achieve goals–this impacts their life stories.

- One adult accepting one child or teen into their home creates a family. Couples can foster and adopt, certainly; but in most states in the US, single adults age 21 or older can be foster parents and adopt, too. And, there's no upper age limit to adopt a child, teen, or a young adult who has aged out of the foster care system–you must pass a medical exam to prove you are physically, emotionally, and mentally capable to parent, but your age is not a discriminating factor.

*Courtesy of Child Welfare Information Gateway (2020). Foster care statistics 2018. Washington, DC: US Department of Health and Human Services, Administration for Children and Families, Children's Bureau. Available online at https://childwelfare. gov/pubs/factsheets/foster/.